LEGENDS OF CHIMA ™

Yannick Grotholt – Writer

Comicon – Artist

New York

# LEGO® CHIMA Graphic Novels Available from PAPERCUTZ™

**Graphic Novel #1**
**"High Risk!"**

**Graphic Novel #2**
**"The Right Decision"**

**Graphic Novel #3**
**"CHI Quest!"**

**Graphic Novel #4**
**"The Power of Fire CHI"**

LEGENDS OF CHIMA
#4 "The Power of Fire CHI"

Yannick Grotholt – Writer
Comicon – Artist
(Miguel Sanchez – Pencils
Marc Alberich – Inks
Oriol San Julian – Color)
Bryan Senka – Letterer
Noah Sharma – Editorial Intern
Jeff Whitman – Production Coordinator
Michael Petranek – Editor
Jim Salicrup
Editor-in-Chief

ISBN: 978-1-62991-155-7 paperback edition
ISBN: 978-1-62991-156-4 hardcover edition

MIX
Paper from responsible sources
FSC® C016245
www.fsc.org

Printed in Canada
February 2015 by Friesens Printing
1 Printer Way
Altona, MB R0G 0B0

LEGO LEGENDS OF CHIMA graphic novels are available for $7.99 in paperback, $12.99 hardcover. Available from booksellers everywhere. You can also order online from Papercutz.com. Or call 1-800-886-1223, Monday through Friday, 9-5 EST. MC, Visa, and AmEx accepted. To order by mail, please add $4.00 for postage and handling for first book ordered, $1.00 for each additional book and make check payable to NBM Publishing. Send to: Papercutz, 160 Broadway, Suite 700, East Wing, New York, NY 10038.

LEGO LEGENDS OF CHIMA graphic novels are also available digitally wherever e-books are sold.

Distributed by Macmillan
First Papercutz Printing

Papercutz.com

FLUMINOX

# The POWER of FIRE CHI

KING FLUMINOX, THE KING OF THE PHOENIXES, IS ABOUT TO DO SOMETHING THAT WILL CHANGE THE LIVES OF LAVAL AND CRAGGER...

AFTER CAREFUL CONSIDERATION, I HAVE DECIDED TO APPOINT THE TWO OF YOU AS BEARERS OF THE MIGHTY FIRE CHI. TODAY YOU ARE TO RECEIVE YOUR FIRST MONTHLY CHI RATION.

USE IT WELL AND--

--USE IT WISELY. MY FATHER SAYS THAT, TOO.

DOES HE REALLY? I'LL SAVE MYSELF THE SACRED WORDS IN FUTURE.

THE PHOENIXES CONSIDER IT A GREAT INSULT IF YOU INTERRUPT THEM.

ROYAL ETIQUETTE HAS NEVER BEEN LAVAL'S STRONG POINT...

LUCKILY, KING FLUMINOX IS IN A GOOD MOOD AND DESPITE LAVAL'S FAUX PAS, HE PRESENTS THE FIRE CHI TO THE YOUNG WARRIORS...

THINGS ARE GOING TO GET VERY HOT FOR THE SABER-TOOTH TIGERS!

YOU BET THEY ARE!

SUDDENLY *TORMAK* AND *LI'ELLA* ARRIVE AT THE HALL WITH A WOUNDED LION...

SLAM

LENNOX!

WE JUST MANAGED TO SAVE YOUR FRIEND FROM THE SABER-TOOTH TIGERS IN THE NICK OF TIME.

THE ICE HUNTERS... ALL OUR WEAPONS AND VEHICLES... NO ONE CAN LEAVE THE CITY...

GIVE HIM SOME *FIRE CHI!* THAT WILL HELP HIM TO REGAIN HIS STRENGTH.

THE LIONS NEED YOUR HELP, LAVAL.

CRAGGER, WE MUST GO TO *CHIMA* AS FAST AS POSSIBLE AND FIND OUT WHAT HAS HAPPENED TO LION CITY.

I'LL COME WITH YOU.

OUT OF THE QUESTION, *LI'ELLA!* IT'S FAR TOO DANGEROUS FOR YOU.

YOU'RE NOT THE ONLY LION WHO'S WORRIED ABOUT HIS TRIBE, LAVAL!

9

HOURS LATER...

HURRY UP, LAVAL. THERE'S NO TIME TO LOSE!

I JUST CAN'T BELIEVE THIS SECRET TUNNEL EXISTS!

I WONDER WHAT OTHER SECRETS MY FATHER IS KEEPING FROM ME.

I WONDER IF LAGRAVIS ALSO KNEW ABOUT THIS!

WHAT--?

SEE FOR YOURSELF!

I DON'T BELIEVE MY EYES! IT'S A VEHICLE GRAVEYARD!

THERE'S MY FIRE LION!

AND MY FIRE STRIKER!

# SIR FANGAR

# FIGHT FOR THE MOTHER TOOTH

TODAY IS AN IMPORTANT DAY FOR THE WOLF TRIBE. TODAY, *WORRIZ* IS TAKING PART IN *FLUMINOX'S* TRIALS IN THE HOPE OF ALSO BEING PERMITTED TO USE THE PRECIOUS *FIRE CHI*...

IT'S BEEN HOURS, CRAGGER. WHAT'S TAKING SO LONG?

PATIENCE, LAVAL. THERE'S NO NEED TO WORRY ABOUT WORRIZ!

WORRIZ! HOW DID THE TRIALS GO?

WELL ENOUGH.

VERY WELL, BY THE LOOKS OF IT. YOU GOT A WHOLE BAG FULL OF *FIRE CHI!*

YOU COULD TOAST A LOT OF MARSHMALLOWS WITH THOSE! OR SABER-TOOTH TIGERS...

MY TRIBE IS PLANNING A PREEMPTIVE STRIKE AGAINST THE ICE HUNTERS. OUR WOLF INTUITION TOLD US THAT THEY WANT TO STEAL OUR SACRED MOTHER TOOTH.

A PREEMPTIVE STRIKE?

BUT YOU'RE NOT STRONG ENOUGH FOR THAT!

WHETHER WORRIZ HEARS LAVAL OR NOT, WE'LL NEVER KNOW...

DO NOT WORRY, *STEALTHOR.* WE HAVE *VARDY.*

VARDY?! SINCE WHEN HAS IT BEEN HELPFUL TO HAVE VARDY ON THE TEAM?

THE VULTURES MAY BE THE MOST USELESS ICE HUNTERS OF ALL ICE TRIBES, BUT THEY ARE THE ONLY ONES WHO CAN TRACK DOWN OUR SECRET WEAPON.

AND HERE HE IS! DID YOU FIND ANYTHING?

THE CRYSTAL YOU ASKED FOR, SIR.

A CRYSTAL IS SUPPOSED TO BE OUR SECRET WEAPON?! WHAT NEXT? EVENING GOWNS AND PEARL NECK-LACES FOR OUR TROOPS?

DO NOT JUDGE TOO HASTILY, MY DEAR STEALTHOR.

MEANWHILE, NIGHT HAS FALLEN OVER CHIMA...

WOW, WITH THAT MUCH *FIRE CHI* WE CAN BLOW AWAY THE ENTIRE FORTRESS!

WORRIZ!

OH, NO. THE KILLJOY COMMITTEE.

THAT'S CRAZY, WORRIZ! YOU CAN'T CHALLENGE THE ICE HUNTERS ON YOUR OWN.

THE FURBALL IS RIGHT. IF IT WAS THAT SIMPLE, THE PHOENIXES WOULD HAVE LAUNCHED AN ATTACK LONG AGO!

LET US DEVISE A PLAN TOGETHER AS TO HOW WE CAN PROTECT THE MOTHER TOOTH!

WE WOLVES DON'T NEED A PLAN. WE WOLVES RELY SOLELY ON OUR INSTINCTS. AND THEY TELL US--

THE NEXT MORNING...

GET ME DOWN FROM HERE, YOU SLEEPYHEADS!

ZZZZZZZZZZZZZZ

WORRIZ! YOU'RE YOU AGAIN!

COULD YOU PLEASE EXPLAIN WHAT THIS IS ALL ABOUT?

...LAVAL AND CRAGGER FILL IN WORRIZ, WHO REMEMBERS NOTHING...

YOU WERE GOING TO EAT US!

OH, COME ON! WE MIGHT HAVE CHASED YOU THROUGH CHIMA UNTIL YOU STARVED, BUT WE WOULDN'T HAVE EATEN YOU.

SUDDENLY, WORRIZ IS TREMBLING IN EVERY LIMB...

ƎUGH...Ɛ THE MOTHER TOOTH... I CAN SENSE THAT THE ICE HUNTERS HAVE IT! I MUST GO...

STOP. THIS TIME WE'RE MAKING A PLAN FIRST.

ALL RIGHT. WHAT DO YOU SUGGEST?

26

GORZON

SOON, AT THE GORILLA TRIBE BASE, A GREAT SURPRISE AWAITS LAVAL AND ERIS...

GREAT. WHY DO WE GO TO THE TROUBLE OF VISITING EVERY TRIBE IF THE PHOENIXES CAN JUST MAKE IT RAIN FIRE *CHI?*

THIS IS NOT THE WORK OF THE PHOENIXES, LAVAL.

IT'S GORZAN WHO IS THROWING HIS FIRE *CHI* OUT OF THE WINDOW!

THE FIRE *CHI* IS A GIFT FROM THE PHOENIXES! YOU CAN'T JUST THROW IT AWAY!

IT'S MAKING OUR ICE FLOWERS MELT, DUDE. WE DON'T WANT IT.

BUT WE CAN ONLY DEFEAT THE ICE HUNTERS AND WARD OFF THE ETERNAL WINTER WITH FIRE *CHI!*

36

41

CRAGGER

LET'S GET OUT OF HERE, LAVAL. I GUESS HER NEW PHOENIX FRIENDS ARE MORE IMPORTANT TO HER THAN WE ARE!

YOU'RE PROBABLY RIGHT...

UNBEKNOWNST TO ERIS, KING FLUMINOX HAS BEEN WATCHING...

HM... IT APPEARS THIS PHOENIX NEEDS TO LEAVE THE NEST...

I HAVE AN ASSIGNMENT FOR YOU, YOUNG ERIS. ACCORDING TO THIS DOCUMENT THERE IS A MIGHTY WEAPON IN THE SWAMP IN THE OUTLANDS WITH WHICH WE CAN DEFEAT THE ICE HUNTERS ONCE AND FOR ALL.

FIND THE WEAPON AND YOU WILL BE A GREAT DEAL CLOSER TO ACHIEVING YOUR GOAL OF BECOMING A TRUE PHOENIX. BUT YOU MUST PASS THIS TEST ALONE. LAVAL AND CRAGGER MUST NOT HELP YOU.

UNDERSTOOD. I WILL NOT DISAPPOINT THE PHOENIXES.

BUT THERE IS SOMETHING KING FLUMINOX SEEMS TO BE KEEPING FROM ERIS...

44

AT THE BORDER TO THE OUT-LANDS, AN UNPLEASANT SURPRISE AWAITS THE HEROES...

MAMMOTHS!

SIR FANGAR ORDERED US TO PATROL HERE.

BUT THERE ARE SUPPOSED TO BE MONSTERS IN THIS PART OF THE OUT-LANDS, MOTHER. EVEN MUNGUS IS AFRAID.

MUNGUS DOESN'T LIKE THE SWAMP.

DON'T BE SILLY, MOTTROT. MY MUNGUS BABY IS AFRAID OF NOTHING AND NO ONE! AND THAT INCLUDES MONSTERS!

BONK

ON THE OTHER SIDE OF THE BORDER...

WOW! I MADE IT!

NOW I CAN FOCUS ON MY MISSION!

MUNGUS MUST FREE MUMMY FROM ROCKS!

YOU CAN FREE US LATER. GO AND GET THE EAGLE. A WOULD-BE PHOENIX IS BETTER THAN NO PHOENIX AT ALL.

MUNGUS HAS TO BE REALLY BRAVE NOW! FOR MUMMY!

I'M AFRAID OUR JOB AS ERIS'S BODYGUARD ISN'T OVER YET.

THE END

54

# WATCH OUT FOR PAPERCUTZ ™

Welcome to the Fire CHI-filled fourth and final LEGO® LEGENDS OF CHIMA graphic novel, by Yannick Grotholt and Comicon, from Papercutz—those chia tea-drinking guys dedicated to publishing great graphic novels for all ages. I'm Jim Salicrup, the de-constructible Editor-in-Chief and part-time librarian for the Phoenixes ! I'm here to take a little look back at all the LEGO graphic novel series available to you from Papercutz.

Of course, it all started with LEGO® BIONICLE. These digest-sized graphic novels featured the great comics that were originally created by DC Comics and were included in the BIONICLE canisters or in the LEGO Fan Club magazine. Every single comics story we published was written by the super-talented Greg Farshstey, including the all-new stories created just for Papercutz. In the Papercutz blog, and in the Watch Out for Papercutz page in BIONICLE #8 "Legends of Bara Magna," Greg revealed the behind-the-scenes story of how BIONICLE was created. In case you missed that fascinating tale, allow me to share it with you again…

"BIONICLE got its start in 1999-2000, when an international team of people employed by the Lego Group were tasked with coming up with a storyline-based LEGO line. The early working title was, believe it or not, 'Bone-Heads of Voodoo Island.' The first story bible (a summary of the year's story) for 2001 actually ended with Mata Nui awakening! No one could be sure if the BIONICLE stories would be big enough to last for more than one year…

"The BIONICLE line was introduced with a comicbook, truck tours, a 'build your own website' contest, and of course, the first six canister sets. The six villager sets (who would later come to be called 'Matoran') were available only through a McDonalds promotion.

"As the Toa were originally planned, they were all different ages and they would all sound sort of 'godlike' when they spoke. I had a long conversation with story team head Bob Thompson as I worked on the first comic, and suggested that the characters might be easier to relate to if they had different personalities, and spoke differently from each other, rather than all sounding like Thor or Superman. He agreed and that's how the initial characters were born in print."

Greg not only wrote all nine of the BIONICLE graphic novels published by Papercutz, he also wrote two in-depth guidebooks to the complex BIONICLES universe, reflecting two very different points of view—MATA NUI'S GUIDE TO BARA MAGNA and MAKUTA'S GUIDE TO THE UNIVERSE. Both profusely illustrated guidebooks were rare examples of books published by Papercutz not containing any comics! With a world as fantastic as the one depicted in the LEGO BIONICLE series, we seriously suspect we haven't seen the last of it!

Of course, Greg then went on to write the hit LEGO NINJAGO graphic novel series for Papercutz, which was incredibly illustrated by PH Henrique and Jolyon Yates. When we look at Garmadon and Samukai, we wonder if perhaps they weren't somehow inspired by the "Bone-Heads of Voodoo Island"! Finally, we also published LEGO LEGENDS OF CHIMA™ written by Yannick Grotholt and beautifully illustrated by the team of artists known collectively as Comicon. We're incredibly proud of each and every LEGO graphic novel we've published and hope you've enjoyed them. If you missed any, you can still find them from your favorite bookseller or as e-books from comiXology.com or other e-book sellers.

From all of us at Papercutz, we sincerely thank you for your support.

Thanks,

*Jim*

Bone-Head of Manhattan Island

## STAY IN TOUCH!

EMAIL: salicrup@papercutz.com
WEB: papercutz.com
TWITTER: @papercutzgn
FACEBOOK: PAPERCUTZGRAPHICNOVELS
FAN MAIL: Papercutz, 160 Broadway, Suite 700, East Wing, New York, NY 10038